Also by Claire Huchet Bishop

TWENTY AND TEN

THE MAN WHO LOST HIS HEAD

ALL ALONE

by Claire Huchet Bishop

Illustrated by Feodor Rojankovsky

SCHOLASTIC INC.
New York Toronto London Auckland Sydney

To Marcel Mermoz,
who was a little shepherd, and
who understands what is in
the hearts
of men

ISBN 0-590-45707-1

Published by Scholastic Inc., 730 Broadway, New York, NY 10003, by arrangement with Viking Penguin, a division of Penguin Books USA Inc.

12 11 10 9 8 7 6 5 4 3 2   2 3 4 5 6 7/9

Printed in the U.S.A.   28

First Scholastic printing, October 1992

Contents

1. Ten-Year-Old Man

"Now, Marcel, you understand—the heifers, they are to graze on our pasture, the one on the Little Giant Mountain. And nowhere else. We don't want trouble with anybody. Is that clear?"

"Yes, Papa," said Marcel.

They were standing in the yard of a farm. The farm was in a valley closely surrounded by the high mountains of the French Alps of Savoie. It was an early morning in the latter part of May. The sun had just touched the peaks around them. The air was light and washed clean. The birds sang. In the farmyard the rooster crowed, the hens cackled, the pig grunted, the cat mewed, and the dog barked as he ran after her. Papa, who wore a walrus mustache, looked down at his ten-year-old son, so small next to the three heifers.

"Remember, Marcel, you are not the only shepherd boy around here. Practically every family has a boy looking after its heifers on one of the mountains during the summer."

"Pierre Pascal is on the Big Giant," volunteered Marcel.

"What? Pierre Pascal? What has he got to do with you? If I ever catch you up there speaking to—"

"I see him in school," said Marcel.

"You see him in school!" roared Papa Mabout. "And what of it? You can't help seeing him in school, can you? Answer me—can you?"

"No, Papa," said Marcel meekly.

"But during the summer it's *my* business, isn't it?"

"Yes, Papa."

"Now, listen. You keep the cows on the Little Giant pasture, and don't talk to anyone—to anyone, do you hear me? And you have nothing to do with other cows but your own. That brings trouble. Don't visit, don't interfere; keep to yourself, mind your own business. That's the best way to stay out of mischief. Get it?"

"Yes, Papa." Marcel sighed.

"And stop sighing," ordered Papa Mabout. "There is nothing to sigh about. I was a boy shepherd too, and none the worse for it. And I was younger than you are. In those days children were not spoiled as they are now. I was nine years old when I went up there all alone with our cows. And Pascal —that is Pierre's father—was there too, on the Big Giant, and he was nine too. And each of us kept on his own. Never even exchanged one word. Why, Grandfather would have thrashed me within an inch of my life if I had done otherwise! He knew! He had been a boy shepherd himself. And he taught me what he was taught: Attend your own cows and nothing else. And now, you do the same."

"Yes, Papa," said Marcel evenly.

"You've got to understand, Marcel," went on Papa more gently. "It's hard to make a living in this part of the country. The land is good in the valley, but each man does not have enough of it in one piece to make it worth while. It is all tiny scattered crop fields. So we have taken to raising a few cows, which, during the summer, can graze on the mountain pastures. The heifers, they are our fortune. And that goes for each one of us in this village who is lucky enough to have some cows. That goes for Pascal too. So we have to watch our cows very carefully. Well, suppose a cow gets hurt. You don't want to give anybody a chance to say it was your fault, do you? So the best way is to keep to yourself and pay no attention to anything else except your own animals. That way you have nobody to blame, and nobody can blame you. See?"

"Yes, Papa," said Marcel, bending down to pet the dog.

"Too bad," said Papa, "that the dog cannot go with you. It would have been company. But high up there it is quite steep, and a dog is no good; he frightens the animals. You've got to be slow and gentle and quiet when you round them up."

Maman came out of the kitchen, carrying a small bag of coarse cloth tied with a long string. "There is a loaf of bread, and cheese and onions," she said.

She also gave Marcel a small wooden cask. That was for drinking water. The cask was made out of one piece of the trunk of a small tree that had been patiently hollowed by hand. It had two iron rings with a string through them. Marcel swung both the bag and the cask over his shoulders. They made him bulge on both sides. Maman paused, briskly bent on her knees so that her face was even with Marcel's and said, "You won't be lonesome up there, will you, Marcel?"

"There, Marie!" interrupted Papa. "None of that. Marcel is a man now, aren't you, Marcel?"

"Yes, Papa," said Marcel firmly, moving away a little from Maman for fear he would start crying, which would not do at all, especially now that the twins, Lucile and Leonard, were just strolling out of the house. Straightening up, Maman said to them, "See, Marcel is going up the mountain with the heifers. You must give him a big kiss. He will be gone all summer."

"All summer!" echoed the eight-year-old twins.

"Sure," said Papa. "Until the fair—end of September. Someday it will be Leonard's turn."

"And mine too," peeped Lucile.

"Stupid!" put in Marcel. "Girls don't go up there."

Lucile started to cry, but Leonard put his arms around her, and she dried her tears.

"Better be on your way, Marcel," said Papa. "Open the gate, children."

Maman clasped Marcel briefly in her arms and went quickly inside the house, wiping her eyes with the corner of her apron. The twins ran to the gate, opened it, and climbed up on it. Papa slapped the cows lightly on the back, calling, "Haro! Haro! Virginia! Geraldine! Haro! Haro! Eunice! Ta, ta, ta, ta!"

"Good-by, Papa," said Marcel.

"I'll take you through the village, my boy, just to make sure you have a good start."

Well, Marcel had not expected that! Mighty nice of Papa. They went through the open gate. The twins swung on it and shut it, shrieking, "Good-by, Marcel! Good-by!" And the dog barked piteously.

The village of Monestier was very quiet—not only because it was very early in the morning, but because it was so far up the valley that there was practically no traffic through it, and, of course, no one in the village could afford a car. People walked, or they rode bicycles, and for the field work they used oxen. The wooden houses, with balconies around the second floors and protruding roofs to protect them from the snow, were old and shabby. The place looked poor and deserted.

There was no one in the street. And yet Marcel knew that, as he and Papa went along, the iron bells of the cows clanging noisily, there was a face behind a curtain of each house, and someone was saying to someone else, "It's Père Mabout and his son Marcel, with their heifers. I bet Marcel is going to take care of them this summer." That's what the Dubois, the Chardins, the Rivars, the Boissiers, the Pelloz were saying behind their curtains. But nobody came out to say hello or to wish Marcel luck. Monestier people were not any different from other peasants; it was just that they had to work so hard to make a living that they had become jealous and suspicious of one another. So gradually they had ceased visiting, getting together. Their motto was "Each man for himself." That's what they taught their children, and Marcel too had been brought up that way.

So he was not surprised not to be greeted on his way through the village. Only he wished he had been. Marcel always hoped life in Monestier might suddenly become different from what it was. The houses he was passing by—he did not know how they looked inside. He wished he did. As he walked along, trying to fit his steps into Papa's, he imagined all the walls of the houses were made of playing cards. He, Marcel, was taking a big breath, and—whoooooofffff! all the cards were tumbling down and he could see the inside of . . .

"Aooch!" cried Marcel, squirming under the grip of his father's hand on his neck.

"What's the matter with you?" asked Papa sternly. "Blowing away like an engine! Enough to scare the cows out of their wits. Daydreaming, getting ideas as usual, I suppose. Don't you do that again, do you hear me?"

"Yes, Papa."

They crossed the bridge of the swift river Isère. Beyond, the road was stony and went up abruptly. Papa stopped. "Here is where I say good-by, Marcel. Keep an eye on Virginia. That heifer, she gets fancies. Don't you let her wander away. When you lead the animals to drink at the torrent, Eunice is apt to trip. Watch out. And Geraldine, she is a great big kitten who loves to play. Stay away from her horns. Somebody will be up next week to bring you a fresh supply of bread and cheese. So long, my boy."

Marcel felt the walrus mustache against his cheeks—one side, then the other. "Good-by," he said in a small choked voice as he turned quickly away. But Papa grabbed him. "Not so fast. Where are your manners? Take off your cap—stand straight, shake hands. Now kiss me and say, 'Good-by, Papa.'"

How hard it was to do all this with such a big lump in one's throat! But somehow, when it was all done, there was no more lump. Papa said—and these were his last words—"Keep to yourself. Mind only your own cows. Stay on the Little Giant. Remember, the heifers, they are our fortune. In your hands, my boy, the family's fortune."

Marcel nodded gravely, and then he was on his way. At the bend of the road he turned and waved. And from then on he was on his own, all alone with the heifers for the rest of the summer.

2. On the Mountain

Slowly they went, up and up. They had all the time in the world to cover the four miles of winding road which led to the pasture of the Little Giant, six thousand feet above the valley. The cows' bells rang clear in the crisp air. Far away

the snowy peaks of the Alps cut a pink lace pattern in the morning light. The valley below with its tiny fields carefully enclosed on all sides looked like a checkerboard. The last farm was left behind, and as they rose in the solitude the cows hastened as if they already smelled the fresh new tender green grass of the mountain meadow.

As they took in one higher turn after another, the sun became warmer. Marcel was getting hot. He took off his heavy black cape, folded it, and slung it on his shoulder. The stones rolled under his thick wooden soles; the sun beat on his head. He almost stopped to take a drink out of the little wooden cask. But no, not now. He would see if he could stand it a little longer—just as far as the next bend of the road, for instance. When he reached it he gave himself another goal, and so on and so on, one hour after another, until at last they reached the torrent, which was bouncing and rushing at great speed. Sweating and tired, but pleased with himself to have stuck to his wager, Marcel led the cows around to a place where the torrent made a detour on more level ground so that it formed a sort of pool. The cows freshened their nostrils in the cool water and drank slowly, while Marcel threw himself flat on the ground and had a few gulps. But he was up again almost at once, and, after having filled his cask with the cold water,

he urged the cows ahead again. This was no time for a long drink; the animals were hot from their climb, and the water had not yet been sufficiently warmed up by the sun.

So they went up and up again, this time to the right of the stream, which had no shade. The left side, covered with spruce trees, led to the Big Giant. After a while there was no path. It was pretty rough going, this dry part of the bed of the torrent. Marcel led the heifers very carefully. As they emerged from the steep slope of the ravine, there was the lovely expanse of the pasture, like a huge delicate green blanket thrown over the back of the Little Giant, gently swaying to and fro under the morning breeze, and punctuated all over with the deep colors of the mountain flowers—the deep blue bells of the gentians, the dazzling yellow of the arnicas, the white velvet of the edelweiss, and the bright red of a small rhododendron bush. And, rising abruptly above, towered the peak of the Little Giant, and far away and all around mountain summits filled the horizon—Ourzan, the Beautiful Star, the Rock, Marcel knew them all. The valley was no more to be seen, and it seemed to Marcel that he was alone high up on the top of the world.

For a moment he stood there in rapture. Then he quickly slid off his cask and his food bag, threw his cape and cap down. He straightened up, looked around as if to take it all in, lifted his head, took a big breath, and opened his mouth wide. "Oloo!—Oo-oo-oo—oop!—ooooo!" he sang lustily. "OOOOOO-oooooooooo" repeated the mountains. And it went on and on, the echo bouncing like a ball from summit to summit. "Oloo!—Oo-oo—ooooop!" sang Marcel, and, without waiting for the echo, he stretched out his arms and began to turn cartwheels all over the pasture. The heifers capered joyously too, and for a few seconds Marcel and the animals danced an impromptu ballet up there, all alone on the mountain, while the echo died down.

The cows stopped; Marcel got up; and as he did so the echo started all over again, as if of itself. Marcel was startled; somebody else must be yodeling too. He scanned the horizon. There was no one to be seen. He listened again. "Oloooo!" Then he was sure: the sound came from the Big Giant, of which he could see but the summit.

"Must be Pierre with his heifers on the pasture," thought Marcel. He felt very happy and opened his mouth to answer. But he checked himself. Papa had said, "Keep to yourself."

"Oloo! le, lo, la le, oop!" sang Pierre again. Then he went on, modulating into an intricate pattern.

"Showing off!" said Marcel aloud. "Phew! I can do that too!" And, filling his chest, he let out a bevy of sounds that went booming, clashing, ricocheting all over the landscape, and to which, of course, Pierre promptly answered, so that before Marcel knew it the two boys were hard at it, outdoing each other in a yodeling contest that became more and more difficult—until suddenly Marcel spied Virginia a few feet from the rim of the mountain. Instantly he stopped singing, his heart in his mouth. Slowly, so as not to get her excited, he went toward her, calling quietly and gently, "La! La! La! Virginia! La! La!" The cow turned her head and, moving away from the abyss, came toward him. He shuddered; a cold sweat ran down his back—a few more steps and she would have been a goner. The family's fortune! He had better attend to his own business indeed! No more yodeling.

He gathered his belongings and went in search of some shade. There was none except that thrown by the little rhododendron bush. He sat there, listening for some more sounds from the Big Giant. But it was silent. Pierre, too, probably was running after his heifers. And now Marcel was hungry. He took out the large dark round loaf of bread from the bag, an onion, and the cheese. He fetched his knife out of his pocket—his stout knife which had been Papa's when he was a boy. He peeled the onion, cut a large slice of bread, and a chunk of cheese. He put the onion and the cheese on the bread, which he held in his left hand, and he proceeded to eat slowly—holding his knife in his right hand, he carefully cut himself a slab of cheese, a small piece of onion, and a morsel of bread. Once in a while he set the precarious tower of food on the grass and took a gulp of water out of the cask.

By the time Marcel had finished his meal it was very hot. He stretched flat on the ground and poked his head under the

bush, trying to get more shade and coolness. It was not very comfortable, but he had no choice.

He was tired and he dozed off. He shook himself quickly and raised his head to look at the cows. He knew cows are always attracted toward the more tender grass that grows on the rims of precipices, and they take one too many steps and fall over and down to their destruction. It would be his main job during the summer to prevent the heifers from going over the ridge. The constant watchfulness would become more and more exacting as the weeks went by and the grass grew more and more scarce. And all the while he would have to be very careful never to scare the animals by quick gestures or sharp commands, lest they run wild and trip to their doom.

But he was so sleepy! Over and over again his eyes closed, and after a few seconds he would open them wide, with terror in his heart. All afternoon, up there all alone in the torrid heat, Marcel fought his first grim summer battle with sleep. He beat his eyes with his fists; he pinched his legs and arms; in despair he took hold of the cask, barely wet his lips, and, stretching back, poured the precious contents over his face. That should wake him up! But after a few minutes his eyelids started to blink again. The struggle was resumed—on and on, endlessly. It was like torture.

At long last the shadow of the rhododendron bush appeared to lengthen as the sun began to dip toward the other side of the sky. A cool breeze swept over the mountain. Exhausted, Marcel got up and collected his belongings. It was time to lead the heifers to drink.

As he started on the two-mile stretch he could not help wondering if Pierre would be at the torrent too with his herd. Marcel hoped he would, then he hoped he would not. Would, would not, would . . . But when Marcel reached the torrent there was nobody there. Perhaps Pierre had not come yet— or more likely he had come already, because he had a longer stretch to cover on his way back to the Big Giant. The heifers drank. Marcel played at throwing pebbles in the water—little ones, so as not to frighten the animals. He washed his face and his hands, took off his shoes, and let his hot feet cool in the torrent. Leisurely he ate his supper, which of course was the same as his lunch; he drank from the torrent and filled his cask. And then there was nothing to do but to go back up again, alone with the three cows, in the silence and glow of sunset.

They reached the pasture as the sun disappeared. Immediately the fog came rolling, way down below, and soon, there on the pasture of the Little Giant, it was as if Marcel stood above a sea of clouds. He was cut off entirely from the rest of the world now. He wished desperately that he were back at the farm. But here he was, all by himself, with the three heifers, on this high mountain pasture, and darkness crept on like a tide. Tears began to obscure his eyes, and he choked with sobs. He could not help it. He was so lonely! And he was afraid too.

And suddenly a faint "Oloo!" struck his ears. He stopped weeping and listened. It rose again, curiously swallowed and muffled by the fog. "Pierre!" thought Marcel, and before he

knew it he had called back, "Oloo!" And for a few seconds
the "Oos Oos" went back and forth from one lonely boy to the
other through the vast solitude, until Marcel signed off with
a short "Oop!" as he saw that his cows were about to lie down.
No time to lose—he made a beeline for them. Geraldine was
down first. He waited and watched eagerly for the two others.
And when Eunice bent on her front knees, quick as a flash he
sprang lightly and landed right between her and Geraldine.
Keplunk! Eunice was down and Marcel was nicely wedged
in between the two animals. He was pleased because he had
timed it so perfectly. He knew it did not always happen. He
had heard Papa tell how one can miss and find oneself out
in the cold for the rest of the night. Virginia stretched on the
other side of Eunice. Marcel was snug and warm. And, since
the singing, he did not feel so lonesome. Pierre too was up
there, all alone, lying between his heifers.

Marcel fell asleep, but several times during the night he was awakened. First it was the heavy breathing of the animals so close to him; then Virginia and Eunice got their horns tangled up, and it made their bells tinkle; and, finally, Marcel had a flea.

The longest stretch of sleep came a little before dawn, but he was pulled out of it sharply by Eunice and Geraldine, who were rising briskly. Virginia followed. On the mountain cows get up as soon as night begins to recede. Just then light was barely perceptible because fog was spread all over, even on the pasture. Marcel shook himself and reached in his bag for a piece of bread. When he raised his head again he could not see Virginia any more. Where was she? Somewhere in the fog. He did not dare move for fear he would get lost himself and not see the other two heifers any more. "La! La! La! Virginia!" he called miserably—and suddenly, in the fog, a monstrous shadow appeared, towering above him, with huge horns, and leaping around. He put his hand on his mouth to stop a shriek as he shook from head to foot. Then a swift form brushed past him. A deer! He laughed as, at the same time, he heard Virginia's bell and made out her shape but a few feet away from him. The fog was thinning out fast. When it had lifted, the cows, of themselves, went toward a crack at the base of the abrupt rise of the Little Giant. There they drank some water which trickled down from melting snow. As for Marcel, he shivered in the cold air. The pasture was covered with dew. He had nothing with which to make a fire. He promised himself he would attend to that this very day. Just then he wished it were already night and he were tucked between the heifers, sleeping on and off instead of having to face that interminable day of relentless watch through the summer heat. But there was no getting out of it, Marcel knew. Such is life.

3. The Dream

Marcel had been up on the Little Giant pasture for a whole week already. Every day had been the same—the heat, the watch, the lack of sleep, and, early in the morning, the cold. Only now at least he could make a little fire after dawn, as there was enough cows' dung to burn. During the day Marcel made the rounds, spotted the dung that was crusty on top, carefully turned it inside out to make it dry right straight through. Then, in the morning he could make a fire. He loved to see the flames going up; they were not only warmth but also life and color, even though the smell was foul.

Of Pierre he never caught a glimpse. But every night, just before the heifers made ready to settle down, Pierre began to yodel, and Marcel yodeled back. It meant "Another day is over. I am here. Good night." That's what the two boys said to each other in their call across the mountain solitude. And each time, afterward, Marcel did not feel so lonesome, and fear receded somewhat from his heart.

Papa came up on Sunday. He brought a fresh loaf of bread and cheese. He guessed Marcel would still have enough onions left, which he did.

Papa slapped Marcel on the back. "Doing all right, eh? You lucky bird! Nothing to do all day long but to look at cows and eat like a king. Think of it! To feast on bread, onion, and cheese every day, three times a day, instead of mush. I would not mind being a shepherd boy all over again myself. Well, I can see we still have our three cows. None of them has gone over the ridge so far, or sprained her ankle, or wandered away. And they seem to fare well. They'll be beauties by the end of the summer. Our fortune, my boy, the family's fortune! By the way, you did not have anything to do with that Pierre Pascal, did you? You did not visit with him, I hope," said Papa with a frown.

"No, Papa."

"And, at the torrent, when you take the animals to drink—?"

"I did not see him. Nobody was there. Ever."

"Good. Just as well. The moment you start mingling with anyone something goes wrong. As I told you before, keep to yourself, attend strictly to your own affairs, no matter what happens pay no attention to your neighbor's business—that's his own worry, isn't it? That way, if anything goes wrong, nobody can put the blame on anybody else, can they? Every man for himself, that's the way we have to be in Monestier."

Marcel did not say anything. He was familiar with Monestier's way. How could he explain to Papa that he, Marcel, felt different? Papa would say it was nonsense. Ideas, he would call it. If Papa knew, for instance, about the yodeling at night, he might even get very angry. Besides, it might sound sissy to him, just as if Marcel were afraid.

"You are not afraid, are you, at night, Marcel?" asked Papa suddenly.

"Not a bit," said Marcel, straightening up and puffing his chest. "Not a bit."

"Ah! Ah! Ah!" roared Papa, laughing. "Your father's son all right, eh? And how! Afraid of nothing, by golly, not even of lying! Ah! Ah! Ah!" And he gave Marcel a big shove which sent him sprawling on the ground. He got up, red in the face and confused, but already Papa was after him again, still chuckling, and they both had a good, rough tussle, tumbling over the grass.

When Papa got up he was serious again. "I have been a shepherd boy up here too, understand? I know. The first season is the hardest. But you'll be all right, Marcel. Well, I have to start back now. Remember—the heifers, the family's

fortune. Good-by, my boy, good-by. Keep it up, keep it up.
Such is life."

Next day, as the sun rose, Marcel noticed clouds gathering
far away, behind Mont Blanc, the highest peak of the Alps.
Gradually through the morning they worked their way up
the sky. The air was heavy and sultry. In the afternoon, when
Marcel tucked his head under the rhododendron bush, the

heat was unbearable, and for a few minutes, try as hard as he could, he was overcome by sleep.

He dreamed that his cows had split in two—two Virginias, two Geraldines, two Eunices—and that he, Marcel, kept running like mad after this suddenly increased flock to keep it from falling off the ridge. Such terror gripped his heart that he woke up shrieking, and as he did he quickly raised his head to look at his cows. His eyes nearly popped out. There were indeed two Virginias, two Geraldines, and two Eunices. He got up, pinched himself. But no, it was no longer a dream; in his pasture were now six cows. Whom did the extra three belong to? Marcel eyed their bells shining brilliantly in the sun. Copper bells! Only Pascal had such. So here were Pierre's cows gone astray. What was Marcel going to do? What was he supposed to do?

Papa's words rang in his ears. "Pay no attention to your neighbor's business." It's his own worry. So the thing to do, evidently, was to shoo Pierre's animals off the Mabout pasture as quickly as possible. Marcel started toward the first heifer. He would shoo them off in the direction of the torrent and trust that they would find their way back to the Big Giant. Probably Pierre was asleep. Too bad. He, Marcel, was very glad that they were not his own cows which had gone astray while he slept. God only knows where they might have wandered, getting lost, spraining their legs, or falling off a ridge. You never knew what could happen to cows left to themselves . . . Marcel stopped short in his tracks. What would happen to Pierre's heifers once Marcel had shooed them off his pasture? Would they go back to the Big Giant? How could he be sure of that? He could not. It was impossible for him to accompany them even so far as the torrent. So there was absolutely no telling what they would do, once alone.

Marcel snatched a blade of grass and, biting it, sat down and eyed the cows. What about his keeping the stray heifers until Pierre came to look for them? He was bound to do so, sooner or later. Later? That was it. Suppose Pierre slept for the rest of the afternoon? Well, it would be a little harder on Marcel—but, just the same, no harm would come to the cows, while if he shooed them off— No harm? And what about their getting into trouble right on the Mabout pasture? And what about Marcel's own cows? Suppose one of them slipped while he was busy with Pierre's cows. The family's fortune! Marcel got up again. Better shoo Pierre's cows off. But that amounted to sending them to their doom. He tried to say that it did not, that whatever happened to them, once off his pasture, was not his business—that it would be Pierre's fault, the result of his negligence. Didn't he, Marcel, know well about it himself? Hadn't he been asleep a few minutes ago? Suppose his own cows had wandered off to the Big Giant?

Marcel went on arguing—to keep Pierre's cows, not to keep them? . . . Papa? Well, after all, Papa had not said anything about what to do in this particular case, had he? One thing was clear—if Marcel shooed the cows off there was but one chance in ten of Pierre's finding them safe and sound; whereas if Marcel kept them— But what about the family's fortune? It was going to be awfully hard to look after six cows. "Well"—

Marcel braced himself up—"I've got to do it. That's all."

It turned out to be much harder than he had expected. It was always nerve-racking to look after the three Mabout cows, but it was nothing compared to looking after six heifers, three of which he did not know, on the relatively small expanse of the Mabout pasture. All afternoon Marcel had to keep a keen eye on them all, anticipating their moves and whims, calling quietly, "La! La! La!" to make them stop, and "Haro! Haro! Ta! Ta! Ta!" to round them up, over and over again, toward the center of the pasture. The dreaded ridge had never looked so near! More than once he was tempted to give up the job and send Pierre's heifers to their fate, whatever it might be. But he did not. He would stick it out, though he was exhausted by the watch and the constant mortal fear that one of the animals would sneak away by herself and fall off the ledge while he was busy with the others. Besides, they were all nervous and fidgety—probably because of the heavy atmosphere, and also because they were not used to one another. Geraldine especially seemed to consider it an occasion for playful scudding about, and she charged Pierre's cows repeatedly, head down. Marcel, trying to stop her, barely dodged her horns several times, and meanwhile all the other heifers got excited and skipped all over the place, to the terror of Marcel, who nevertheless had to keep his wits about him and firmly but gently call them and quiet them down.

And still Pierre did not come. It was a harrowing afternoon for Marcel. It seemed to him it would never end, that it had been going on forever. It was like a nightmare.

As the day wore on and Pierre did not appear, Marcel's anxiety grew. He would have to take it upon himself to bring the whole herd down to drink, and what a ticklish job that would be! He decided that the best he could do was to give himself plenty of time to go down. He would start much earlier than his usual time. It would make no difference to Pierre's cows, who probably were used to an early drinking time, since Marcel had never met them at the torrent and the way back to the Big Giant was much longer than the stretch back to the Little Giant. And as for his own heifers, with the heat and the excitement of this afternoon they too would welcome the chance to go down sooner. Yes, that was the best arrangement, he thought. If he waited until his usual time, and Pierre had not showed up, he still would have to take the whole herd down to drink—but then it would be too late to do it leisurely, and Marcel did not trust himself to handle the whole herd quickly when going down the steep bank.

He had no difficulty in rounding up the animals. They were indeed all very willing to go down. Carefully, slowly, his heart in his mouth at every step, Marcel took the herd down the two-mile stretch. And all the while his anxiety mounted. Would he meet Pierre? And if he did not—? When the pool came into view he was scared to look at it. And when he did Pierre was not there—but there was a cow drinking; and as Marcel came down he saw she had a copper bell. What a relief! It was Pierre's cow! Pierre must be not far away— probably looking for his other cows upstream and worrying to death. Marcel wanted to shout—but no, he would keep

quiet and give Pierre a big surprise when he came back.

Marcel eyed the cows with pride and joy. Here they were, Pierre's cows, safe and sound—and, for that matter, so were the Mabout cows. Nobody seemed the worse for helping. Of course it had been a dreadful afternoon, but Marcel had well nigh forgotten it as he stood there, surrounded by all the cows. There were footsteps across the bank, and Pierre appeared, wild-eyed, an intensely worried expression on his face. All of a sudden he caught sight of his heifers. He shrieked happily, waved his hand, and started to run. Marcel smiled back broadly and extended his arms as if he were taking in the whole herd. And as he did so Pierre seemed to check himself; a dark look spread over Pierre's face, and as he slowly reached the other side of the pool his mouth was set and his eyes hard.

"So," he snarled, "you are the one who took my cows?"

"I did not take them!" retorted Marcel. "They came over to my place."

"Everybody knows that kind of story," sputtered Pierre. "You just managed to lure them away, didn't you?"

"I did not!" protested Marcel, indignant.

"You did!" shouted Pierre.

"I did not!"

"You did! My father told me right—that I should have nothing to do with you."

"*My* father told *me* right—that I should have nothing to do with *you!*"

"But you did, didn't you? Are my three cows with you or aren't they?"

And with that, both boys bent down quickly, picked up

small stones, and started to throw them at each other. They ducked, picked up new stones, threw, ducked again. Pebbles, aimed short, rained into the water. The drinking cows raised their heads, splashed around uneasily, bumped into each other. And suddenly Eunice slipped. "Oh!" shrieked Marcel, stopping abruptly, a stone in his hand. He let it go at once as he rushed to Eunice. Gently he led her away, out of the water, eagerly watching her feet. No, thank God! She was all right. He shuddered—the family's fortune! Anger swelled within him. He turned around and faced Pierre, who had remained motionless, a stone in his hand, on the other side of the pool.

"You silly fool!" shrieked Marcel, shaking his fist. "See what you are doing? I wish I had shooed off your dirty cows when they came to my place. My father was right! It does not pay to lend a hand; you always get the blame. I wish I had let the darned animals wander off by themselves and lose their way—and break their necks, for all I care! But I warn you, don't ever fall asleep again, because there won't be any next time with me for your ill-starred beasts. If I ever set eyes on them again in my pasture you'll never get another chance of finding them with me. I'll shoo them off all right, and no mistake. Take back your precious cows, and go back to sleep, you good-for-nothing soft sissy shepherd!" And Marcel spat into the torrent. Then he called his own heifers, turned his back, and started to climb up the slope toward the Little Giant.

"Wait!" cried Pierre as he gathered his strength, jumped

clean over the pool, and landed next to Marcel. "How did you know I was asleep?"

"Leave me alone!" grunted Marcel, walking on.

"Why did you do it?" went on Pierre, stepping on beside him. "Why did you not shoo my heifers off? It was your right to do so! Everybody in Monestier would have done so. In fact, you *should* have done so. Why didn't you?"

"You were asleep," grunted Marcel again, still walking on.

"How did you know I was asleep?" asked Pierre, putting himself squarely in front of Marcel.

"You asked that once already," said Marcel impatiently, trying to bypass Pierre. "You just can't guess, can you?"

He raised his angry face toward Pierre. The boys looked at each other—and they burst out laughing.

"Go back to sleep, you good-for-nothing soft sissy shepherd!" chanted Pierre with a twinkle in his eyes. And they both laughed again and pushed each other away playfully.

"Listen," went on Pierre, "it was mighty good of you. Mighty good. Nobody else would have done it. Nobody." He extended his hand. Marcel took it. "I nearly went crazy when I woke up and found three out of four gone. Never expected to see them again, except maimed or dead. Must have been awfully difficult to look after so many on your small pasture— and how did you manage to bring them all down?"

"That's why I had to start so early," said Marcel.

"Yes," said Pierre, "that was the only safe thing to do. Well, *mon vieux*, thanks, and if you are ever in trouble you can count on me too. Say, you don't yodel badly at all. I've had more practice at it because it's my second year up here. But you are good."

"Really?" asked Marcel, beaming. "About yodeling—and everything else—I won't tell my father—"

"'Course," said Pierre. "I won't tell mine either, cross my heart. It's between us boys. Grownups, they never understand— What's that?"

Far away, an ominous rumbling sounded.

4. The End of the World

"A storm," said the two boys at the same time, looking anxiously over the ravine. The sky was black. Lightning zigzagged, tearing the clouds.

"No wonder," said Marcel, "it was such a sultry afternoon. But I had no idea the storm was so near. I and my animals had better get back in a hurry to the Little Giant."

He turned toward his cows, only to find them faced about and going back down toward the pool.

"La! La! La!" he called, but already they had splashed through the water and joined Pierre's cows, who had also gone across and were standing there under the trees with their heads turned toward the Big Giant.

"Come on, Pierre," said Marcel quickly. "Help me to get them back."

"It's no use," said Pierre. "They won't come. Not now. The animals feel what is coming. Look, the storm is moving fast from the east. In a few minutes it will sweep over the Little Giant. If you and the animals were still up there, as you would be if you had not had to bring my cows down, you would have time to make ready for the storm. But to go back now is impossible; you would have to face the hurricane, the animals might get lost, and you might be blown away. Better wait here where we are somewhat sheltered."

"But—" began Marcel.

"Listen!" interrupted Pierre sharply.

They heard it coming from afar. First a tremendous wail, louder and louder, and then a roar like a storm at sea. They ran down the slope none too soon, jumped over the pool, and joined the herd. The fury of the elements broke loose, the wind buffeted the ravine as with a giant's fist, bent the trees like pieces of straw; and almost immediately pelting rain slashed through the leaves. Against a tree, their capes spread over their heads like tents, the two boys huddled against each other, peering through the rain at the motionless backs of the animals, thinking how lucky they were to happen to be in the shelter of the ravine, which offered them some protection from the violence of this severe storm.

But their feeling of comparative security did not last long, as suddenly they heard in the distance a booming sound like a cannon. Pierre grabbed Marcel's hand, pulling him away and yelling in his ear in a terrified voice, "The torrent! The torrent!"

Marcel needed no further explanation. He understood at once what was happening. The storm had swollen the stream

in the higher regions, and now the water was coming down,
like a tidal wave, at top speed.

Quick! Quick! Through the blinding rain the two boys
urged the herd up, away from the ravine, toward the open
pasture of the Big Giant. The animals' instinct helped them;
they too sensed the mortal danger behind them. They all
climbed in haste out of the temporary shelter of the ravine.
Just as they reached the open space a deluge of angry water
catapulted into the ravine behind them, tearing trees, sweep-
ing rocks, and filling the whole gully in a second with bellow-
ing whirling foam. Had they delayed a few moments, boys
and herd would have been carried away.

And now they were pushing their way up toward the
pasture of the Big Giant, driven foward by the wind on their
backs, and blinded by the rain. The thing to do was to find
some hollow in the side of the mountain and wait there for

the end of the storm. Pierre led the way, and Marcel brought up the rear. The boys went on, heads bent, gasping for breath, hugging close to the mountain so as not to be thrown down. Just as it seemed to them they could not take another step they found themselves around a contour of the mountain and somewhat protected, by its protruding flank, from the force of the wind. The animals huddled close together, their heads away from the wind. The two boys crept behind them and leaned against the wall of the mountain. As the storm's rage mounted and mounted, they squatted down on their haunches, hiding behind the large bodies of the animals. They moved close to each other, searching for each other's hands under their capes, and grasping them with all their strength. Lightning came so fast that it was like a continuous curtain of fire; rain poured like waterfalls driven by the wind; the mountains roared, boomed, snapped at each thunder clash as the echo went crashing against each summit. Noise increased every second. It was everywhere—around, in the air, and underneath in the earth, which grumbled and growled. Then came a tremendous blast, which shook everything; it was as if all was set in motion. Terror-stricken, Marcel and Pierre clung to each other; their teeth chattered, water ran down their faces, and they did not know it was tears—nor could they hear each other's sobs.

How long did it last? They never knew exactly, as they had no watch, but when, shortly after the last crash, the noise gradually died down and the storm moved away, they were surprised to see that it was still daylight. Pale and worn out, they got up. The animals moved slowly away from the makeshift shelter. Marcel and Pierre shook themselves, stretched, and flapped their arms. In the cool air they moved stiffly around. And now the sun shone brightly, and the boys, exhausted and stunned, looked around with blinking eyes at the whole landscape, which seemed all fresh and new.

"What's that?" asked Marcel, pointing to a cloud of dust slowly drifting away from the top of the Little Giant.

"That's it," said Pierre. "I mean the awful racket we heard a little while ago. Some big rock must have split somewhere in the storm and made quite a bit of dust."

"Lucky the wind has shifted," commented Marcel, "or else it would have blown down on us. We have enough worries as it is. How long do you think it will be before I can go back with my cows over to the Little Giant?"

"It all depends," said Pierre, "how big the cloudburst was upstream. It may take a day or so for the water of the torrent to recede. Maybe more. We don't know."

Marcel stood there, speechless. Papa's words rang in his ears—"Have nothing to do with other cows but your own. That brings trouble." Sure enough, there it was. Because he had taken charge of Pierre's stray cows he had gone down sooner to the torrent, and now he was stranded and marooned. And suppose Papa came up the Little Giant to see how Marcel had fared in the storm? A cold sweat ran down Marcel's back. He felt sure Papa would be coming, probably tomorrow . . .

"Come to think of it," went on Pierre, "you did me more than a good turn by keeping my cows and not shooing them off. If you had, with that storm coming so fast, they surely would be lying down dead at the bottom of some abyss by now. But they are all right—and as far as you and your heifers are concerned, you just stay here with me on the Big Giant for the time being."

"Stay here!" Marcel gasped. "And Papa likely to come tomorrow to the Little Giant, after this storm!" He tucked his head between his shoulders as if warding off a blow.

Pierre's face clouded. "I didn't think of that," he said. "It goes for *my* father too. Likely he will be coming up too. And if he does and finds us here together—oh, boy! oh, boy!"

It was unnecessary to say anything else; the two boys understood each other. They knew what to expect, and in this fearful anticipation they forgot their recent terror in the storm. But things were as they were; Marcel could not cross back with his cows that evening—that much they knew. Perhaps tomorrow, if they were lucky. Meanwhile with one accord they moved on toward the pasture on the Big Giant.

It was a large pasture. Marcel and Pierre took off their water-soaked capes and spread them on the ground. "Suppose we eat," said Pierre.

"What do you have?" asked Marcel dispiritedly.

"Bread, onions, and hard sausage," said Pierre.

"My!" exclaimed Marcel, his mouth watering.

"Yes, can you beat it?" asked Pierre. "My father brought it to me last week. Because I passed my graduation exam. Quite a treat, eh? And good too. Mother made it. Wait till you taste it. I sort of saved it. I ate all my cheese first."

"I have some cheese we can share," said Marcel.

"But it's a regular banquet!" shrieked Pierre.

It was, and in the enjoyment of it the boys' spirits rose, and they forgot their worries.

Later, after each of them had tucked himself successfully between two lying heifers, Pierre called, "Marcel! It's wonderful not to be alone."

"Yes," said Marcel. "If only we could herd together always! But my father would never be willing."

"Mine would not either," said Pierre. "Nobody would, anyhow, in Monestier. It is every man for himself."

"Yes," commented Marcel. "That's true. Grownups—they are queer. What do you suppose is the matter with them?"

"Nothing," said Pierre. "They are just grownups, that's all. We will be too, someday."

"No," said Marcel firmly, "I won't. I mean, not that way. When I am a man I'll say to everybody in Monestier, 'Let's do everything all together!'" He opened his arms wide in a large gesture. "Ouch!" he yelled.

"What's the matter?" inquired Pierre.

"In talking I spread my arms and struck the cows' sides, and they slapped my face with their tails."

Pierre laughed. "See," he chanted, "already your fancy ideas are getting you in trouble!"

They were quiet for a while; then Marcel asked, "Are you afraid?"

"No," said Pierre. Then he added, "Not tonight. Are you?"

"No," said Marcel. "Not tonight." Then he added, "We don't have to yodel, do we?"

"No," said Pierre. "We can just say good night."

"Good night, Pierre."

"Good night, Marcel."

5. Prisoners

In the morning, after the sun had cleared away the mist, the two boys decided that Marcel would stay with the cows while Pierre went to find out the condition of the torrent, since he knew more about it than Marcel.

When he came back he began to shake his head in a "no"

motion long before he was near Marcel, and as he approached Marcel noticed how upset he looked. "What's the matter?" asked Marcel.

"The torrent—" said Pierre in a frightened voice. "The torrent—it does not flow in the same place."

"What?" cried Marcel.

"No," said Pierre. "There is still a lot of water, but that is nothing—nothing. It's the place itself." He grabbed Marcel by the shoulders and shrieked, "There is no more slope on the other side of the water. There is a cliff—a high, steep cliff!"

"A cliff!" echoed Marcel, wide-eyed. "You are dreaming! There never was a cliff there!"

"There never was, but there is now," said Pierre. "Something happened."

"It's impossible!" cried Marcel.

"You go and see for yourself," said Pierre.

Marcel did. When he came back he sat down heavily on the grass and buried his head in his arms. Pierre came and sat beside him, patting him on the back. "You saw it, did you?"

Marcel nodded. They were silent. Marcel raised his troubled face between his hands and whispered, "How am I ever going back to the Little Giant now?"

"You can't," said Pierre. "Not that way."

"There is no other way from here," wailed Marcel, "except—" He started to cry.

"Except to go down to the village and up again," finished Pierre.

"And I will have to pass in front of our house, and my father—"

"It's tough," commented Pierre soberly.

Marcel went on weeping. After a while, Pierre seemed to make up his mind and he said soothingly, "Stay here with me. The cows are all right."

"Stay here!" exclaimed Marcel, drying his tears. "And your father coming up here, and mine looking for me on the Little Giant! No thank you! I prefer to get what's coming to me right away. If I stay, that will only make matters worse. As a matter of fact, I had better get started now and get it over with. The sooner the better."

He got up, slung his bag and his cask over his shoulders, and called, "Haro! Haro! Virginia! Eunice! Geraldine!"

"I'll put you on the path going down," said Pierre heavily. He walked with Marcel and the cows to the end of the pasture. They stopped.

"It's all my fault," said Pierre. "You must tell your father. If I had not let my cows go astray, you would still be on the Little Giant now. It's my fault."

"I don't regret anything," said Marcel.

They shook hands sadly. "Good-by!" called Marcel as he disappeared around the bend of the steep path.

It was a much longer way down to the village from the Big Giant. Down and down they went, each step bringing Marcel nearer his father's wrath and causing his fear to mount within him. He tried to steel himself against it. It would be but a bad moment. It would pass. And after all, were not the cows safe? But he knew that even this would not ward off his punishment. He pictured himself telling his father that he had been at the torrent so early because he had taken care of Pierre's stray cows all afternoon. He could already hear his father shouting, "And if Pierre's cows had been hurt while they were with you? And what about ours? Never occurred to you that on that small pasture it was mighty dangerous to have so many cows, did it? What did I tell you to do? What was your job? Pierre's cows or *our* cows? Our cows! Our family's fortune! but Mister did not care—he had ideas as usual. I'm going to trim your hide in such a way that ideas get out of your skin forever."

Yes, it would be somewhat like that, what Marcel was headed for. He clenched his fists and yelled inside himself, "I don't care! I don't care! I'd do it again if I had to!" He quieted down, relieved by his outburst. What he had just said to himself he could never tell his father. That he knew. He would have to go through the whole ordeal and not say a word. Well, he could take it, but when he was grown up he would speak up—and not only to his father but to the whole of Monestier, just as he told Pierre last night. "Let's do everything together." That's what he would say boldly, and then . . .

The animals in front of him came to an abrupt stop. What was the matter? The path was narrow and wound like a corkscrew around the mountain. Marcel had not turned one of the corners yet, so he could not see what had caused the animals to stop. Cautiously he made his way ahead along the ridge of the mountain, in order to pass the animals and discover what stood in their way. And as he did so he stood petrified with horror. There was no more path ahead. It was entirely blocked by masses and masses of huge rocks. They filled the entire width of the narrow path, and not only was it impossible to get by them—since on one side was the wall of the mountain and on the other side a sheer drop—but one could not tell how far the road was blocked because, since the path kept winding, it was impossible to see ahead. It might be a few yards or it might be several miles. But whether it was one or the other made no difference to Marcel and the cows. They could not pass. There was nothing for them to do but to go back to the Big Giant.

For the time being all Marcel could think of was the extreme difficulty of making the animals turn around on this narrow ledge and retrace their steps. Backing was out of the question; it would be far more dangerous. Marcel walked to Virginia, who was the first in line. He took hold of the collar of her bell and, gently talking to her, he led her around slowly, he himself walking all the while on the edge of the abyss. Then he came back and did the same—first for

Geraldine, then for Eunice—and though he was a mountain boy, used to height and danger, yet he did not relish this walking on the outside of the path with a big animal that had to be led carefully. But at last it was done, and they all were on their way back up, slowly.

As they approached the pasture, the iron "hello" of the cows clanging in the air, Marcel heard a call and looked up. It was Pierre, stretched flat above the ledge. "What's the matter?" he shouted.

"Path's blocked!" answered Marcel.

"Blocked?" repeated Pierre.

"Landslide!" called Marcel.

"*Ah, mon Dieu!*" said Pierre.

They were trapped—boys and cows—on the Big Giant. They could not reach the village one way or another. They were marooned, cut off from the rest of the world. Right there in the open, in the bright sunshine, they were prisoners. The Big Giant had become a fortress from which no escape was possible.

"They are bound to discover what happened," said Pierre

later. "Someone—my father, probably—coming up to see how I and the cows fared in the storm."

Marcel did not answer. It was terrible to be cut off from the rest of the world, but in addition—to be stranded on somebody else's pasture! All because you did not attend strictly to your own business, trouble had started and did not seem to end. Marcel wished he were now at home with the cows, getting the beating due him, instead of having to wait for it in this awful situation which made the whole matter ten times worse.

All that first day the two boys listened eagerly for the sound of a pick or shovel, or a human voice. It would mean their predicament had been discovered. But they heard nothing. Over and over again they took turns at walking down to the blocked area on the path, only to come back more downhearted. There was no sign of any rescuing party. They also went back to the torrent, which had somewhat receded, and walked upstream, trying to find a passage back to the Little Giant. But there was none. The cliff rose on the other side, high and forbidding, preventing any attempt at crossing. The day dragged on endlessly. At lunch the two boys decided they had better have only one meal a day in order to save food, since they did not know how long they would be stranded. At night, heavy-hearted, they curled up between the heifers.

When they awoke on the second day hope filled their breasts. Surely someone would be coming. Again they listened all day and ran often down the path. But nothing happened. In the evening, after they had led the cows to the torrent to drink, Pierre suggested they make a fire. Perhaps the smoke would be seen from the village if the wind blew in that direction, and somebody might guess they were in trouble. He had a pile of cows' dung which he had collected before the storm. But it was none too dry after the rain, and the boys could not get a spark out of it.

"I can't understand it," said Pierre on the third evening. "My father should have come up to see how I fared in the storm."

"My father must have gone to the Little Giant, and he did not find me," said Marcel.

"Maybe he went to the torrent," suggested Pierre, "and he saw he could not get down there because of the cliff. Say, Marcel, that makes me think, if you had been on the Little Giant you would not have been able to get to the torrent after the storm. You'd have had to go back home with the heifers."

"Sure," said Marcel.

"Then," asked Pierre, "why did you worry so much about taking them down the other morning? You would have had to anyhow."

"But," said Marcel, "the other morning I had to go in through the other end of the village, coming from here, so Papa would have known right away that I was not coming from the Little Giant."

"Can't fool him, eh?" said Pierre.

"No. And that's just what makes it so awful for me now— not only that I am stranded, but that I am stranded here on the Big Giant, where I have no business to be."

"I know," said Pierre. "And all because of me. You saved my cows but you got yourself into hot water. It is just as people say in Monestier—keep to yourself, or else you get yourself into trouble."

"I don't care," said Marcel fiercely. "I don't care. I'd do it all over again! Cross my heart, I would!"

"You're not like anybody else. No mistake. You're not like anybody else," said Pierre, shaking his head.

They were silent for a while. Then Pierre said, "Let's make another fire; the cows' dung is dry tonight."

They did. But then the wind came, and the smoke drifted in the opposite direction from the village.

Only on the fourth evening did the fire burn well in the still air, but a heavy fog spread below, so that the signal was use- less. The two boys sat looking at the fire and fanning it. But it failed to cheer them up. The vast solitude and the unbroken silence had become unbearable to them. They felt caught, held in the grip of an evil power all the more terrifying in that it was nowhere to be seen and that they seemed to have retained freedom of movement.

"I am frightened," said Marcel in a low voice.

"I am too," said Pierre.

"It's awful," said Marcel. "Everything as usual—the sun, the night, the animals. And yet us here—prisoners, right in the open."

"Ghastly," said Pierre.

"Perhaps they have forgotten us," went on Marcel.

"Perhaps we will stay here forever," commented Pierre.

"I'll tell you," whispered Marcel gloomily. "I think we are dead. Already dead. That's what I think. Dead."

Pierre opened his eyes wide. "I know," he said. "We are like that man the teacher read about in school. He was an American. His name was Monsieur Rip van Vanq', and he went to sleep on a mountain, and when he was found he was a hundred years old."

"He must have had an awfully long beard by that time," said Marcel thoughtfully.

"He did," said Pierre, "and long white hair too."

Marcel caressed his cheeks and chin. "Do you suppose," he inquired, "we too will have beards when they find us?"

"It all depends how long it takes them," said Pierre.

"Yes, it all depends," echoed Marcel sadly.

The sun rose and set on the fifth day, and still nothing happened. They had used all the dry cows' dung and could not make any fire.

The sixth day came. It was Sunday. Surely someone would appear! It seemed impossible that no one would. But Sunday went by like the other days.

A new week was ushered in, and the boys were still alone. They gave up going down to the path. They had begun to

feel weak from lack of nourishment, and from worry. All day
they lay down. In the evening they dragged themselves to
the torrent for the sake of the cows, which still had to be
looked after. Coming back from drinking, the contented animals started to graze, as if everything were as well as ever.
It was, for them. For the time being what difference did it
make to them whether the boys were stranded or not? They
had food aplenty. Watching them, the boys felt envious, re-
sentful, and anger rose within their frightened hearts as,
ravenously hungry, they sat down to their own scanty meal.
Suddenly they flared up at each other.

"You have more bread than I have!"

"Mind your own business!"

"You have eaten some of your cheese on the sly!"

"I did not!"

"Liar!"

"Liar yourself!"

They went rolling over the grass, pummeling each other and trying to tear each other's bags.

"It's *my* bread!"

"It's *my* cheese!"

The strings snapped. The bags went flying across the field. Marcel and Pierre, scrambling to their feet, saw them sailing through the air toward the rim of the mountain. Wildly the two boys ran after them, flopped down flat on the ground, and snatched the bags just as they went over the ledge—the boys themselves were nearly pulled over and down by the jerk. They crept to their feet, each holding one bag. And, as they looked at them, they saw—Marcel held Pierre's bag, and

Pierre held Marcel's. They had rescued each other's bags. They eyed each other sheepishly, and suddenly, in spite of their exhaustion and their anxiety, they began giggling softly, and, without saying a word, arm in arm, they went toward the place where they had built their fireplace with a few stones. They had had the same idea—they would put all the food together between the stones.

"From now on," they said, "it's for both of us. The whole thing. We eat it together. It is *our* bread, *our* onions, *our* cheese. It is *our* food."

These were brave words for the very little that was left. They did not want to think of the time when there would be nothing at all.

As it was, they went to sleep very hungry. In the middle of the night Marcel began to have nightmares. In his sleep he gave out a piercing shriek that woke Pierre up with a start. He heard the echo repeat Marcel's cry. On and on and on and on it went, like an endless answer—an answer. "A fool answer," thought Pierre bitterly, shaking his fist at the mocking sound. But the echo was not dying down! Pierre sat up abruptly. Strained and tense, he listened. And suddenly he was sure. It *was* an answer!

"Wake up! Wake up!" he shrieked, running to Marcel. "Wake up! Do you hear? Listen! Listen! They are coming."

"Oloooo!" sang the mountain. Holding their breath, the boys waited until the echo died down, and then they called back. "Oloo! Oo! Oo!" And again the answer came. Why had they not thought of it before? They had been so frightened and hungry that they had not yodeled once since the storm.

They stood there in the night, on the pasture of the Big Giant, shivering with excitement.

"Let's go down."

"No, we can't," said Marcel. "There is no moon. It's too dark. It would be dangerous."

"Tomorrow they will be here. We are saved! Saved!"

They fell into each other's arms and hugged each other. And at the same time each asked, "Are you hungry?" They laughed, ran to their cache, and ate all the cheese, all the onions, and most of the bread that was left, saving just a small piece of crust—for breakfast, they said grandly. And after that they fell asleep right on the spot.

6. The Least Expected

As the cows got up and light spread over the mountain range, the boys woke up and heard the call again. "Oloooo! Oo!" And joyfully they answered.

"You know what?" said Marcel. "It's more than one person calling."

"Perhaps it's my father and your father together," said Pierre. "Why don't you run down and see?"

"No, you go," said Marcel.

"Why not you?" asked Pierre.

"Because—if my father is there—and here I am—on the Big Giant—"

"But," said Pierre, "if he is, he has probably already recognized your voice when you yodeled."

"That's true," said Marcel. "Just the same—now that we are going to be rescued—I don't feel in such a hurry—"

"Perhaps he won't beat you," suggested Pierre sympathetically. "By now he may have forgotten what he told you."

"Forgotten!" exclaimed Marcel. "You don't know my father. He never forgets anything."

"Mine does not either." Pierre sighed. "Well then, I'll go down."

He was not gone long. When he came back he was very excited. "I could not see anybody," he said, "because the path makes a bend. But I called, and my father's voice asked, 'Are you all right, Pierre?' I said, 'Yes.' And then another voice sang, 'Where is Marcel?'"

"Bet it was my father's," commented Marcel. "What did you say?"

"'All right,' I said. 'With me.'"

"That's a big help!" wailed Marcel.

"Well, I had to," went on Pierre. "But listen. After I said

that there was a cheer, as if there was a crowd of people. Can you beat it? A crowd of people! They must all be working together at clearing the path."

"Then it won't take so long," said Marcel.

"No, it won't. I bet they get here today. My! Will I be glad! That crust of bread was not much this morning!"

The whole day they heard the sound of picks and shovels, and once in a while a call would ring through the air and they would answer it. But they were so tired that by noon, when the heat was at its height, Pierre fell asleep. Marcel kept an eye on the cows and on the path. He too was exhausted, but he could not have slept even if he had not had to watch the cows—he was too worried. At last he heard the

shuffling of many feet below. He shook Pierre. "Wake up! They are coming! Lots of them! Must be the whole village!"

They stood up, holding each other's hands. Pierre whispered fiercely, "I won't let him touch you!" And together they faced the entrance of the path. But before anyone had appeared that way, suddenly behind them there was a noise. Over the ridge one—two heads, and then two figures, hoisting themselves up with strong and quick movements of their bodies, straightening up, and running toward the boys with open arms.

"Papa!" shrieked Marcel and Pierre together.

And there they were, held fast in the powerful embraces of their fathers and kissed over and over again. Then more and more people were around them. And there was Maman Mabout, weeping and crying, "Marcel! My Marcel!" And she clasped Marcel in her arms and showered him with kisses. And she did the same to Pierre. And then they were handed over from one to another, hugged, pushed, smacked, shaken, and kissed, until all was a blur in front of their eyes and they turned very pale.

"The poor darlings!" cried Maman. "Let them go! They are hungry! Where is my basket?"

Somebody handed it to her, and out came fresh-baked bread, hard-boiled eggs, and—could it be possible?—rabbit pâté, which is a very special delicacy. The boys' eyes bulged, but when a cake came out, a real *gâteau de Savoie*, Marcel and Pierre gave up. "Cake!" Neither one could remember when he had last had any. It happened once or twice a year, on very special occasions. What did it all mean anyhow? Of course they had been stranded. But just the same— And how come the whole village was making so much of them? There was something so unusual about all this. And what about that scolding for Marcel, which had not come off?

"Marcel," said Papa, "when I went to the Little Giant—"

"Ah, here it comes," thought Marcel, already making himself very small.

"—and did not find you there . . ." went on Papa Mabout. He stopped, shook his head, and asked, "How did you get out of there, Marcel?"

Marcel cleared his throat. "I was at the torrent. With the cows," he said.

"What?" queried Papa. "At the torrent? How come? It was far too early at the time the storm came to take the cows down."

"I was there," repeated Marcel stubbornly.

"But why?" insisted Papa.

There was no way out of it. Marcel had known it all along. Sooner or later the truth would have to come out. He braced himself. But before he had a chance to say a word, Pierre blurted forcefully, "It was my fault! My fault!"

"Your fault!" exclaimed Papa Pascal.

"I must say I can't understand anything!" said Papa Mabout.

"He had my cows," said Pierre, speaking very fast. "I had fallen asleep. They went astray. On the Little Giant. Marcel did not shoo them off. He figured out they would be killed. He looked after them—the whole afternoon." That was hard to say. "He took all the cows together down to the torrent earlier, because he could not manage that many quickly. It was my fault."

He hung his head, and so did Marcel. But no blow followed. Instead all was so quiet that a fly could have been heard. In the silence Maman said in a choked voice, "A miracle! A miracle!"

Marcel felt Papa's hands weighing on his shoulders. He stiffened. Papa said slowly and sadly, "You'll never take the cows to graze again on the Little Giant, Marcel. Do you hear me?"

"Yes, Papa," Marcel obediently acquiesced, head still down and his heart beating wildly.

"There is no more Little Giant pasture," went on Papa Mabout heavily.

Marcel raised his head inquiringly. "No more Little Giant pasture?"

"No," said Papa Mabout. "It has been wiped out. Entirely. Landslide. And to think that here you are, alive, safe and sound. Oh, my boy!" Papa Mabout pressed Marcel close to him.

"Yes," said Maman. "Think of it, Marcel! The Little Giant pasture gone! We nearly went crazy when we discovered what had happened. When your father went up and saw tons of rocks, and the mud, and you nowhere, it was only too plain that you and the cows were buried under. What else could have happened?" She broke away, crying, *Mon petit! Mon petit!*

"There, there, Marie," said Papa Mabout. "It's all over. Here he is, a little shaken, but alive. Had he not gone down sooner to the torrent because of Pierre's cows, he would be no more. And now he is all right."

"And so is Pierre," rejoined Papa Pascal, "and so are the cows. All the cows, yours and mine. Mine too. Your son did it, Mabout. He did it. So suppose you take the boys down now for a good sleep at home, and for the time being I'll look after the whole herd."

"Thanks," said Papa Mabout, "but this is not my pasture. I have no more pasture. I had better take my animals away."

"Nonsense," said Papa Pascal. "This is the least I can do for you now."

"He is right!" cried everybody. "Pascal is right. Take the boys down, Mabout. And don't worry about anything."

So Maman left her basket of food with Papa Pascal (there was still a lot left in there), and everybody started on the way down.

As they went they explained to the boys why it had taken so long to rescue them. After the storm the river Isère had flooded the valley, carrying away all the bridges; and its angry water, running over at great speed, had made it impossible to cross for a week. Papa Mabout was the first to attempt it. He was terribly worried, not only on account of Marcel's being short of food, but because, like everyone else, he had seen the cloud of dust rising over the top of the Little Giant after the storm. When Papa Mabout came back he ran through the village like a madman, shrieking, "The mountain fell! The mountain fell!" He made such a racket that everybody came out, including Papa Pascal, who was just about to start on his way to the Big Giant with food for Pierre. "The mountain fell!" raved on Papa Mabout. "You can't even get near to it any more! My boy! My boy!"

"Let's try to get at it from the Big Giant," Papa Pascal had said.

"You could not have," interrupted Marcel. "There is a cliff now on the other side of the torrent."

But that, of course, the people of the village did not know at the time! They grabbed picks and shovels and went up, only to find the path of the Big Giant blocked with huge fallen rocks for a stretch of two miles. So everybody started working like mad to clear the road. Perhaps that was the reason no one had tried yodeling. They were too busy. Or perhaps they were afraid of receiving no answer and of knowing Pierre's fate too. For, as far as Marcel was concerned, nobody entertained the hope of ever seeing him again. And yet Papa Mabout worked like a Trojan to clear the path. He never said a word until the last night, when the call of the boys was heard.

"Papa sat down and wept, they tell me," said Maman.

"Think of it, Marcel! Papa weeping! And he said, 'Someone
go and tell the Maman.' That's what he said, bless his heart.
And when I heard, I ran to Maman Pascal. I could not help it,
and I told her. And she said, 'You bring the twins here, I'll
look after them. And you go up there to see your boy. And,
wait, you take with you that cake I have just baked in case
my Pierre would be coming home today. You take it, for
them both.'"

It was a happy crowd that went back to Monestier—everybody talking to one another and going over and over the story. Maman went to fetch the twins at Madame Pascal's, and of course there the story had to be told over again, and Pierre and Marcel hugged and kissed all anew. Lucile cuddled against Marcel. "I don't want to be a shepherd on the mountain, ever!" she said. "You don't have to," said Leonard soothingly, and he put his arms around her.

By and by everybody went home, each one shaking hands warmly. "Good-by, Dubois, good-by, Chardin, good-by, Rivar, good-by, Boissier, good-by, Pelloz, good-by . . ." "We must talk about all this again," they said. "Soon! Let's get together!"

As for Marcel, he was asleep even before he had reached his bed. He was so very tired.

7. The New Way

"Do you remember, Pierre?"

"Do you remember, Marcel?"

It was just a year after the mountain fell. Marcel and Pierre were walking through the village. They were dressed in their Sunday best, though it was not Sunday, and the whole street

was decorated as for a festival, with gay-colored fanciful arches. Who would have recognized the old dour and sad Monestier? People dashed in and out of their freshly painted houses, hailing each other joyfully and calling, "Eh there, Marcel! Eh there, Pierre!" And the boys waved. "Good day, monsieur! Good day, madame! Good day, mademoiselle!" they called as they passed by the houses that were no longer a mystery to Marcel. He had been inside all of them during the year. He thought, "The walls of the houses, they were made of playing cards after all, and they tumbled down. I don't have to go 'whoooooofffff' any more."

"What's the 'whoooooofffff' about?" teased Pierre, laughing and poking Marcel in the ribs. "Getting ideas again? Lay off and look! Isn't it pretty?"

They had reached the square, and it was so beautifully decorated that it took your breath away—nothing but flowers and ribbons and flags and Chinese lanterns. The crowd was gradually filling the space, and there was much noise and excitement. Above the din you could hear the voice of the ice-cream vendor, calling, "Who does not have his ice cream? Ask for ice cream! Chocolate, vanilla!"

"Shall we have one?" asked Pierre. "I have some money."

"So do I," said Marcel. "But let us wait till after." And he pointed to the middle of the square. There stood something like an elephant, so big it looked. Only you could not tell what it was because it was all covered with a tarpaulin.

On one side of the square there was a platform, where the band had taken its place, and also a few other people.

"Eh there, boys! Come on up here!" called someone from the platform.

Marcel and Pierre looked all around to see who was being called.

"You two there!" said the voice again. "Marcel Mabout and Pierre Pascal! Come on up. We are waiting for you to start!"

It was no one less than the mayor, *Monsieur le Maire*, beckoning to them from the platform. Well, Marcel and Pierre certainly had not expected that! "Isn't it lucky that we haven't bought our ice cream cones yet!" whispered Pierre to Marcel as they went up.

Papa Mabout was there too, and Papa Pascal, and other men. And now the mayor nodded to the leader of the band. The band struck up the popular air "Les Montagnards," the Mountaineers, and everybody joined in lustily. Then the mayor got up.

"Citizens," he said, "I'll try to be brief. But this is a great day for Monestier. We don't want to forget it—ever. What stands there in the middle of the square, under the tarpaulin, is going to remind us of it for a long time to come. But even

that won't be sufficient to make us remember what made such a day possible. We've got to remember *what* happened and *who* made it happen.

"First, *what* happened. A year ago in Monestier, as you

recall, it was every man for himself. Each one of us looked after his tiny scattered fields and his few cows the best he could. It was hard to eke out a living that way. So we were afraid of each other, and each of us would have nothing to do with the other fellow. Correct?"

"Correct," acknowledged the crowd.

"And what's worse," went on the mayor, "we were proud of being like that, all alone. We called it being on our own, independent, having no account to render anyone. We said that what was good for our parents was good enough for us.

"But times had changed, only we refused to see it. I dare say that if anyone had so much as suggested that the sensible thing to do was to get together and pool our resources he would have promptly received a punch in the nose!" (Laughter.)

"And here we are today all gathered together. All of us are going to take a step, which, I dare say, is going to change even the look of this valley. The land of our valley is good, but it has been going to waste for a long time. Why does it not feed us any more? The trouble is that each man's fields are too small and too scattered. That's what we ourselves figured out as we talked it over all together, time and time again, when we met at one another's homes during the past winter evenings. And finally we came to a momentous decision. Of our own free will—" (Applause.) "Yes, of our own free will, without anyone telling us to do so, we, the people of Monestier, have decided to tear down the age-old fences and hedges which enclose and separate our fields, and to work the whole land of the valley together—one common field under the sun." (Applause.)

"That's what we have decided. How it can be done best we will have to figure out among ourselves. We know it's not going to be easy. It's quite an adventure. There will be plenty of discussing, arguing, planning, organizing. It will mean a lot of hard teamwork all around for every one of us. But it will also be great fun. We know we are on the right track, because we are in this voluntarily, all together, touching elbows and feeling the beats of one another's hearts." (Applause.)

"That's *what* happened, citizens. But now we come to the second and most important question. *Who* made it happen?

"Some people might say that it was all because the mountain fell—that in time of danger or calamity people get together who never did before. And that is true enough. But, citizens, you know as well as I do—mountains, floods, earthquakes, fires, diseases, and wars fall on men. For a short time everybody works with everybody else, everyone is friendly, generous, and kind. Then everybody forgets.

"For us, too, the mountain could have fallen in vain, and our rescue work together be but a memory. We could still be the old Monestier, resembling many other dying French villages where people keep to themselves. But we are not. Why?

"Why? Because what counts is not the fall of a mountain but what is in the heart of man. So someone must have lit the spark. Who did? Did I? Did you? No!

"A little child did it. If it had not been for this one"—and, to Marcel's utter confusion, the mayor pulled him up and pushed him in front of the people—"if it had not been for Marcel Mabout, we would all still be crouched in our own dens, peering at each other from behind curtains." (Laughs and applause.)

"A little child showed the way, the new way of life. How did he do it? It was all very simple. Cows from a neighbor went astray on his pasture. What did he do? According to Monestier's old custom, he should have shooed them off at once, washing his hands of what might happen to them later. They had no right to be on his pasture, and if anything happened to them while they were there he would be blamed. Of course, if he had chased them off it was ten to one that they would wander and break their necks. But it was none of his concern; it was the neighbor's, whose fault it was for not watching them properly." Here Pierre squirmed in his chair.

"Marcel knew all that, and yet he did not shoo the cows off. He took care of them right on the spot, and we can all easily imagine what it meant and how difficult it was. Why did he do that? He thought of his neighbor, later finding his heifers dead at the bottom of an abyss. And though, in keeping watch over the stray cows, Marcel, mind you, endangered his own, his family's, fortune, yet he decided to run the risk.

"Citizens, a little child took charge of his neighbor! That's what it amounted to. That was Marcel's great idea!

"You know the rest—how his friendly gesture not only saved all the cows, but also turned out to be his own salvation, and, I might add, ours too. Because that's what set us to thinking. It was an eye-opener to us. We began to see that there is a better way of life than each man for himself and the state for all. We began to see that if we would get together of our own accord, life might be better in Monestier. And we did get together, and one thing followed another, and here we are today, celebrating, so to speak, the resurrection of our village. That's what it is—the resurrection of our village. And the resurrection came from a child's heart. That, citizens, is what we should not forget—ever. A little child led us.

"Marcel"—and here the mayor stepped next to Marcel—
"Marcel, I shake hands with you, in behalf of all Monestier
people—you, who made us discover a new way of life."

There was a thunder of applause and shouts of "Bravo!
Bravo!" Marcel was quite overcome and embarrassed. When
the noise died out his small voice rose shyly in the square.
"Monsieur le Maire, thank you very much—but—it's not I.
It's Pierre. He was the one who started yodeling in the eve-
ning. And his 'oo, oo'—and his 'oo, oo, oo'—and his—"

Everybody laughed. Marcel was very red. But the mayor

said roundly, "I get it!" and he pushed Pierre in front too, calling loudly at the same time, "Hurrah for the boys! And off with the covering!"

Twenty hands fell on the tarpaulin and drew it off. And there was a brand new shining tractor, a Massey-Harris, with which they all could work their land together.

Everybody crowded around the tractor. Marcel and Pierre edged their way among the people. "Listen," said Marcel to Pierre, "isn't it funny, it's just as I said—'let's do everything together,' you remember, that time on the mountain, when

the cows' tails struck me?—Ouch!" he cried as the powerful hand of the mayor gripped his neck and he was carried away and set down on the seat of the tractor.

"*Vive Marcel!*" shouted the twins, Leonard and Lucile, jumping up and down frantically. Maman wept. Papa threw his cap in the air. And everyone reached for another's hand and formed a ring, dancing around the tractor, and all, including Marcel, joyfully sang the old French folk song:

Ohé! Ohé!
Let us change hats
And drink
The health,
The health,
Of the com-
Of the com-
Of the community!